Are You Busy Friday?

Con todo mi cariño y
admiración

(Lots of love and
devoted admiration)

[signature]

2014

Núria Salán Ballesteros

© 2013 OmniaBooks, Omnia Publisher SL
1st Spanish and Catalan edition: April 2012
1st English edition: September 2013
ISBN: 978-84-941447-0-7
LD: B-23158-2013
AMPERSAND
http://www.ampersand.es

© Cover Art: Khrees Illustration&Design
© Cover Design: Joan Rodó Amat

Dedication

To my daughters Anna and Eva,
who have given me the gift of being a mother.

"One is not born, but rather becomes, a woman."
Simone de Beauvoir, 1908-1986

"Live in such a way that nothing you do merits the reproach or condemnation of those around you."
Simone Weil, 1909-1943

" I am grateful to fate for three gifts:
having been born a woman,
of lower class
and oppressed nation.
And the turbid azure of being three times a rebel."
M. Maria Mercè Marçal i Serra, 1952-1998

Acknowledgements

I would like to give very sincere thanks to all of the Marias who have crossed my path in life and have thereby nurtured me and helped me to grow.

To all of the women in my family, for having helped me to design the lifestyle I have as my model today.

To my friends at Can Jordana (Sant Boi de Llobregat) for encouraging me to write and for always being there "on the other side." To all of the women I have worked with, everywhere I have worked, because they have shown me how to be a woman and how to get along with women.

To my friend Pilar (Pi), because she is always up for reading what I write.

The author

Contents

Foreword

Perhaps humankind is not so different from the rest of its neighbors on the planet, especially other animals. We are predators in every sense of the word; we are weak when circumstances overwhelm us and bold when we feel secure. In addition, our need to communicate with each other is as vital as is breathing. And this is the key to everything...

Núria Salán communicates with sublime control; she does so avidly and with a special charm. Of this I have no doubt. But the most remarkable thing is that in this work, *Are You Busy Friday?* she invites us to live and share with its main character a story that reflects very well what 'communication' means.

Times change, and we have also done so against our will and swiftly. Postmen or mail carriers, intermediary figures of information and messages, have been cardinal in the history of our society, still today performing tasks that require their existence. Nonetheless, a new, virtual conduit for relating and communicating with each other has scaled the ranks of interaction —one we will seemingly never again be able to live without: email!

Imagine the "sent" folder of anyone you don't know—imagine the stories and misadventures this electronic sentry guards, and very jealously, revealing them only to the account holder or chosen recipient to whom they are sent at the speed of light—letters that form words with a life of their own and phrases that seek to have their own voice, messages that are very often more emboldened when typed on a keyboard than when sender and receiver are face to face, feelings that occupy a specific place and come to life in their turn, as they cannot be governed by any sort of disciplined schedule.

If we also possess creativity, a sense of humor and the author's ease with words for portraying the truths— sometimes sweet, sometimes bitter—that surround us, we find this: a story I will always remember as a modern fable that hooks you from the start and draws you into an intimacy, a life and characters that might seem invisible but who remain with you throughout the story.

The cast of the book you are reading is original and appealing, and it beckons you to delve in and follow where it leads you. So much so that this foreword will take up no more of your time and I invite you to commence. Get comfortable—you are about to be trapped in Núria Salán's web, but don't fret, she spins with heart and intelligence. She moves you without harm, and that is only within the reach of a few.

Enjoy your read and congratulations on such a fine choice!

Amadeu Alemany. Sant Boi, April 2012

Subject: Are you busy Friday?
Date: 11 May 2010, 20:00:25 + 0100
From: Maria <marieta@mail.com>
To: Juan <juanitu@mail.com>

Hey Juan!!!!

Do you want to do something on Friday? I looked at what's showing in the movie theaters and there's some good stuff on...

Ramon can't come with us this time—he has a business meeting that wasn't planned. This husband of mine, poor thing, is working more and more, but look, this isn't the time to be saying no to business meetings, and even less so to go to the movies. He did say that if he can he will come find us in the shopping center after the film is over and have dinner with us.

The truth is that he's really overwhelmed. He works terrible hours, comes home tired and hardly feels like doing anything. I'm afraid that they're pulling a fast one on him at work and he doesn't want to tell me so as not to worry me. You know he has always tried to keep me out of his problems at work, but, I can tell that he is worried. And I also worry.

Just to give you an idea... A couple of weeks ago, I called him around half past eleven because he hadn't come home or said anything to me, and it turns out that he had put on a watch that didn't have the time changed. So, he thought it was an hour earlier than it actually was. Can you imagine how absent-minded he is? When he got home, he saw that all of the clocks had the "old" time, like his watch... because I had changed them all. For a minute he just stood there opening and closing his mouth, looking at his wristwatch... But my face gave me away. He lowered his head and went off to change, muttering and shaking his head. I had to change all of the clocks again, but I laughed for a good while. Lol!

Well, anyway, surely there's nothing to worry about—it will all be a temporary situation that goes by without further incident, and I am sure if he knew I was telling you about this he would tell me I think too much about stuff. He's always laughing about the "stories" and worries my head harbors.

And speaking of my head! I went to the salon and let them talk me into getting my hair cut. Not much (or that's what I thought), an inch in all, with some layers, to change things up a bit. Ramon noticed when he got home and said it suited me but asked me to please not cut much more off, he's so fond of my long hair ... Man, it made me feel bad an all. In truth, I've worn my hair long for so long that I wouldn't know what else to do with it, but from time to time I give in to my hairdresser's styling temptations... Anyway, since we're going to see each other Friday you'll see that it was just a 're-styling,' don't get me wrong...

Well, now it's your turn. Let me know if Friday works for you and what time you'd prefer to meet. If the choice were left up to me, I'd be more partial to the 7:30 session—that way it won't be too late when it's over and we can have a relaxed dinner, and Ramon should be done around half past ten and can join us...

Let me know! Maria

Subject: YOU'RE NOT GOING TO BELIEVE IT!
Date: 14 May 2010, 16:10:35 + 0100
From: Maria <marieta@mail.com>
To: Juan <juanitu@mail.com>

Juan!!!!!!!!!!!!!!!!!!

I'M GOING TO ROME!!!!!!!!!!!!!!!

Yes, yes, yes!!!!!!!

Oh my God, oh my God, oh my God, my heart is still racing... Man, it was one of those things - wham, bam! - that you don't think much about. No plan, no warning, no nothing...

I called to tell you but you didn't pick up and I couldn't wait to tell you about it. I am eager, enthused, excited... I don't know, this is all new for me. And I am also scared, of course—it's the first time, THE FIRST, that I am going away alone, without Ramon, and since I met him everything I have seen of the world has been with him (and before that, having been hardly anywhere, well, I hadn't been anywhere). And, really, I still don't believe it... Oh my god, oh my god...

I still don't believe it... I still don't believe it...

Wait, let me take a deep breath and I'll explain...

I've sometimes mentioned a group at work that looks for travel deals from time to time and goes away for a long weekend (taking an extra day off, Friday or Monday). Well, it's not a set group either; it's more or less the same people, but now and then there is someone who's gone once but not the

5

other times... And the thing is I have never taken part in one of these trips. Not for any particular reason—I don't have a problem with anyone, not at all - it's more that I like to take my vacations with Ramon; with the people from work I'm happy having a coffee in the morning, the Christmas drink and not much else—I've always kept personal time separate from work. So a few months ago they started organizing a trip to Rome for the weekend of the local festival, taking the holiday (which falls on Thursday this year) and the Friday in between. Me, like I said, I didn't put my name down to go because it didn't even cross my mind. I kept hearing them talk, about the trip, Rome, museums, shopping and so on. But I hadn´t said anything to you because it wasn´t my thing.

So what happened is that one of the girls from work can't go. Well, it's not actually that she can't, but that she doesn't want to, poor thing, because she's suffered a blow... Apparently her husband told her a few days ago that he was leaving because he'd met another woman and all that, and my colleague, who was crazy about her husband, is taking it very hard, the poor thing. I don't know her very well, just from work, coffee breaks and the Christmas drinks and not much else, and she seemed to have a very normal relationship. But look, everything fell apart for her in no time ... She hasn't been to work in days, since it happened, and the girls say it's because it's hit her really hard; she doesn't want to go outside or see anyone. And naturally she doesn't feel like going anywhere, much less traveling...

And, of course, they had already made her reservation, and everything was paid. And one of the women from work asked if we knew anyone who would want to go, not to let the reservation go to waste—today the name could still be changed and the whole package used, and at least she would get her money back, not that it's much since they found a really good deal, but that's what one of the girls who organized the trip was saying...

And that's when Ramon called to say hello, and I said something to him about the woman and her husband and the trip and stuff. And he goes and says that I could jump on it and go with the people from work. And I just stood there with the phone in my hand because it hadn't even crossed my mind. So anyway, Ramon started to tell me that he would probably be working until late on Friday and it looked like Saturday morning too, and he felt bad that he and I wouldn't be able to go anywhere and I would be stuck at home all 4 days. And I didn't say anything because I didn't know what to say. And then he said that it would be good for me to go because that way I could start to have a look around Rome, where to go, where to stay, what to see, and that it would be a big help to him for me to go "ahead" because he had been thinking we could go this summer but would have wanted to tell me as a surprise... Sooo sweeeet!!!

Anyway, he talked me into it, and when I told the girl at work that if it was ok I could take the "vacant" spot, everybody was taken aback—not for any reason but because I had never gone with them, but, look, they changed it today and I came home with the reservation in my bag... AND IN TEN DAYS I'M GOING TO ROME!!!!

My, I am super nervous—I already said so, right? I don't know where to start; I'm waiting for Ramon to get here to show him the reservation and the papers they gave me at work and everything... And I got my suitcase down, and I started looking at what to put in it and what not since I ONLY HAVE 10 DAYS!

Well, I'll see you tomorrow, right? I'll tell you about it then, and I'll give you details about the trip, where they want to go, where we're staying and all of that...

Aaaaaaaaaaaaaaaarrrghhhh! I'm a nervous wreck!

I'll stop there, Juan—I want to start looking around to see if I have everything I need. I don't want any last-minute surprises or rushing or racing or frights or anything else!

I think I've repeated myself, but I'm not going back and deleting... You can delete it yourself. (Lol!)

Oh, my nerves!

See you tomorrow!

Maria

Subject: Did I leave my scarf in your car?
Date: 17 May 2010, 18:15:30 + 0100
From: Maria <marieta@mail.com>
To: Juan <juanitu@mail.com>

Hi Juan!

Have you found a scarf in your car? I can't find the one I was wearing on Friday. Well, I could swear I was wearing it... It's a patterned foulard with a very striking label (that's exactly why I didn't remove it, because it was striking), and Ramon gave it to me for our anniversary last October... I must have left it on the backseat because I left my bag there when you brought me home... And I could swear I was wearing it, I can picture having seen it in the car...

But since I've been going through ALL of my clothes to pack my suitcase for the trip, maybe I'm mixed up and maybe I wasn't wearing it on Friday and here I have you looking in the car... Man, I'm a mess... I didn't tell Ramon I can't find it; I don't want to upset him. Anyway, I'm sure it will turn up, in your car or around somewhere...

Let me know after you've had a look.

Listen, Ramon wanted me to thank you for bringing me home and thanks for going to the movies and dinner with me (when you see him, tell him I told you so he'll know I did).

Poor thing, he got home after midnight. He hardly ate dinner because they'd ordered sushi (and he's so grossed out by raw fish, poor thing) and he was wrecked. I started to tell him about the film we saw but he couldn't keep his eyes open and I left off... The next day he told me he was very sorry to have missed the movie. And dinner with you too, of course...

This job is going to be the end of him. But look, like he says, "we have to plough with these bulls," so if that's what he has to do now, it's not the time to be difficult about work...

Actually, from what he's told me, I don't think he'll be around for several weeks—he'll be all tied up on Friday afternoons/evenings; you know how before the summer everyone wants to leave things squared, and they schedule things by the week, so he has to make sure everything is done on Friday.

Well, what looked like it was going to be a one-off week of extra work coinciding with the local feasts and my trip to Rome will not be so out of the ordinary... But it's just for now, he said, not forever... Precisely now, with a couple of complicated weekends ahead, family get-togethers and his nephew's daughter's communion. Poor Ramon, he's not very good with these things—you know how he has never liked family celebrations or things with too many people around; if on top of that he's swamped with work and tired, I can imagine how reluctant he'll be...

And truthfully, I suppose we all change over the years, but this husband of mine, over the last few years he has become more and more "private" as I say, and since he has his work buddies who play squash every week and all he's been less into meeting up with his cousins. And even less with his nephews and nieces—kids overwhelm him and he ends up with a headache.

And look, now that I've brought up his squash buddies: since there are more and more people and they play in a "league," he's stuck on the "bench" more often, and sometimes the shirt in his bag isn't even sweaty. But being as he's so dependable, poor thing, he never fails to show up. There are days I think they are doing a number on him because they all pay the courts together whether they play or not and the ones they go to are not exactly cheap, and since they know that he always comes I suppose they count on him as someone who will pay for sure.

He says that he almost always plays, but I suspect this is not the case because I see his clothes in the hamper and they often look like they haven't even been unfolded. You can imagine how much he must have played! One day I was on the verge of telling him not to bring the bag back if his stuff wasn't dirty, but I didn't because I watched him as he unpacked his things and it seemed like he was sad, and I thought that if I said anything to him he would be more "affected"—I didn't want him to see that I know that they are taking him for a ride... And man, what can I say, if he's all right with that...

Well, anyway, we'll be in touch, and I'll see you either way, with or without Ramon. It will be after I get back from Rome, though, but maybe before your name day ideally, and I can tell you how it went...

And about the trip, I almost have my suitcase packed (I ONLY took 5 days to pick everything out, haha). Man, you'd think I'm going away to summer camp and not for a long weekend...

You want to know something? My heart is very divided... Part of me is really excited about the trip and everything, and the other part of me feels horribly guilty... I'm going and leaving poor Ramon here all by himself with work. I know he's going to have a lot of work and won't be at home much those days, but I feel bad that he'll come home to an empty house and have to sleep alone...

Well, it's better not to think about it, or I'll change my mind at the last minute... And the part of me that wants to get away is very insistent!

Let's go! I'll call or write in a few days!

And tell me if you've found the scarf! I get so into what I'm talking about and I nearly forget why I was writing you...

AND I'M GOING TO ROME IN 4 DAYS!!!!

Man, oh man, oh man, I am getting old (haha).

Take care of yourself.

Maria

Subject: ETERNAL ROME!
Date: 24 May 2010, 19:24:22 + 0100
From: Maria <marieta@mail.com>
To: Juan <juanjuanitu@mail.com>

Juan!!!!

I'm back from ROME! We have to get together, I brought you something! And you'll have to suffer through the photos I took along the way (haha).

I don't know where to start! It was pretty good, actually. The people from work, they are very friendly and organized—they made proposals and everyone voted on them. And whichever option was chosen, everyone accepted it readily... The truth is that they're a pretty nice group to take that kind of trip with. I would never have imagined...

And the hotel was an excellent choice, honestly... In the end the hotel staff asked if we would switch two double rooms for a triple (a double with an extra bed) and a single because they had a last-minute thing (the truth is that I didn't understand everything because what with this Italian man shouting like a madman, gesticulating and swishing his arms about like a windmill and making a great fuss like he needed somebody to whip him, the reason for the change wasn't all that clear to me; what was clear is that it was necessary). So they offered to let me have the single room since it was the first time I had come along, in case I wanted more privacy and all... And listen, I was very appreciative, because I was really a bit worried about sharing a room depending on who it was with... Well, so I felt like a queen.

We used public transportation and it was a little bit crazy, but there were a couple of people who seemed to have spent their whole lives there and they were able to tell us where to get on, where to get off, where we needed to switch. I tell you, it went really, really well.

I'll tell you about where we went when I show you the photos; you know how I like to have them printed, and I'll put them in an album and show them to you the next Friday when we go to the movies—let me know when you're free and what you want to see. And if it's ok, I was thinking that one day I could ask someone from work if they felt like coming to the cinema. But only if you like the idea, and I don't mean every time, just once. It's like everyone was so nice I feel indebted to them.

I even had one of those moments that seems like it's out of an Almódovar film, man, with a museum guard—I don't know what came over him... Look, I'm even embarrassed to tell you the story... But maybe it's better if I tell it here; if I have to tell you and see you laugh I will be mortified...

So we went to visit the Borghese Gallery, which is in the center of Rome, a villa, lovely, and we're all there looking at the artworks and statues. We come to a Bernini statue, and as we'd seen the Ecstasy of Saint Teresa the previous day, in a full swoon as if George Clooney had declared his love, I don't know what was going through my head since I have NEVER done things like this, but I go and pose like the statue... Well, I throw back my head, put my hand on my breast, make a face like I'm losing my head and let loose a sigh... But nothing was wrong with me; I just wanted to be funny...

And here comes the museum guard, thinking I've gotten dizzy. Everything happens in a split second: he goes and pushes the people aside, grabs me and begins to shout, "Non si preoccupi! Mi occuperò io della signora!" and I'm trying to stand up and I was so dumbstruck that not a single word escaped my mouth, not one! I wanted to tell him that nothing was wrong with me, but this man had whisked me up with his hands like claws (and believe me, I thought he must have had many more than two, because I felt them frisking me all over) and there I am trying right myself and both of us end up losing our balance and whoops! We're both on the floor! Well, I'm on the floor and the guard is on top of me—I don't know what kind of first-aid maneuver that was... Trying to get him off me, I start to kick the air and yell because I couldn't move my hands, and thinking I was having an attack, the guy gripped me even tighter.

Can you imagine?

Seeing all of this, the people from work - since I'd never played a joke- are all looking puzzled at the scene, until someone reacts and pulls this dude's tentacles off me... I thought that I would never get out of there again, Juan... What an awful moment...

And when I managed to free myself from the guard, we were all in such a state. I felt like bursting into tears, and everyone else was trying not to burst out laughing. At that moment I would have come home, I swear... But one of the ladies, who couldn't help smiling, came with me to the restroom and let me be alone for a while. Look... When I rejoined the group, everyone laughed openly about the "show", and from the outside looking in I myself thought that it must have been quite a comedy show...

And when I told Ramon about it, at first I thought it had made him mad because he got very serious and told me that I deserved what had happened, that I am a temptation for museum guards, that the poor man, the guard, will still have trouble keeping his job... And I didn't know what face to make, and then he starts to laugh and tells me how very sorry he is to have missed it... And he told me that when we go to Rome this summer we have to return to the museum to see if the guard is still there and pull that number again to see what happens. What a joker Ramon is... But I'll see to talking him out of going back to that museum. Not a chance...

Anyway, apart from this "incident," the rest was great, great, great. Did I mention that it was great? Haha.

And when I got home, poor Ramon told me that he was away almost all weekend—he got home late on Friday and on Saturday as well. And on Sunday he slept in very late; that's why he didn't answer the phone that morning... Imagine if he was rested and relaxed that when we got to the airport I had to wait for him for a good while. Nearly everyone had left and someone had offered to take me home; I was very appreciative, but I had to wait for Ramon... Poor thing, he wasn't paying attention and arrived nearly an hour late, but I was pleased he came to get me to be honest...

Now, when I have the photos printed, I can tell him about the plan I had in mind for our vacation... Rome is a fantastic city, and if I get to go with Ramon it will be even more so. What I will look into is getting a hotel that is a little more central— the one we stayed at this time was way out on the outskirts, even though the information said it was "central"... What a cheek the Italians have!

Well, I'm home now, and in a couple of days I will have finished doing ALL the laundry I have to do (just 4 days, eh, and it's as if the world had ended...) and when I have everything back in order I can resume my life.

And we're free on Friday if you want to meet up. Wherever you say: cinema, theater or a musical. Your choice. And expect the two of us—I'll see about cajoling Ramon into coming even if he just manages to make it on time. Otherwise he'll just have work and more Work and that won't do.

I look forward to hearing from you.

Maria

Subject: Change in plan….
Date: 3 June 2010, 19:14:15 + 0100
From: Maria <marieta@mail.com>
To: Juan <juanjuanitu@mail.com>

Hey Juan!

I expect you'll have already gotten the tickets for tomorrow. I'm sorry to spoil our plans, but we can't come.

Please tell me how much our tickets were and I'll pay you back and you can take whoever you want with you—weren't you saying you wanted to tell your sister and her husband to come? Invite them to go with you and you'll have made out like a king… But just to be clear, I'm paying you back for them, OK?

Nothing's wrong, but yesterday Ramon wasn't feeling well and he isn't looking too good today, so tomorrow I'll try to keep him home in the afternoon, see if I can convince him not to go to work, and we'll have a quiet evening—I think he really needs it.

I just wanted to tell you that, and now I'm off to the kitchen; I want to make him whiting for dinner, and I want to prepare it well, boneless—he won't eat fish otherwise - Choosy or what!

But I'm not complaining; he's not feeling well today, poor thing…

Speak to you soon!

Maria

Subject: We won't be able to meet up...
Date: 17 June 2010, 16:54:18 + 0100
From: Maria <marieta@mail.com>
To: Juan <juanitu@mail.com>

Hey Juan!

It looks like we won't be able to meet up this week either. Ramon still isn't up to par; he says it's nothing, that it's fatigue, but he has been looking unwell for days and I wouldn't want to leave him at home alone and much less to go to the movies...

He insisted, he told me to go with you, but I would rather stay. And I'm really sorry about it—I was reading up a little about the film you mentioned and was really into seeing it...

I tried to call to tell you myself, but I couldn't reach you. And I know I can tell you this way, but I felt like talking to you and telling you that I'm a little worried about Ramon. You know him, and you know that he has always been reserved, but lately he has been very gloomy. And since he's so apprehensive, I don't dare say anything to him... Well, surely I'm overdoing it.

Now it turns out they're going to have to work on Friday afternoons no matter what. Until now if it was necessary they stayed, but if everything was wrapped up by lunchtime they had Friday afternoon free. But now, since his boss is Swedish and single, Ramon says he has nothing better to do than work and he has scheduled the weekly meeting for Friday afternoons. Can you imagine? Ramon says that he will live with it for now, over these weeks, but that if it goes on like this after vacation he will set things straight with whoever it takes...

And when I hear him say that, it makes me worry he might have a problem at work... With the way things are, it's no time to get into arguments with anyone, much less the boss... Well, let's see if he simmers down a bit...

Hey, I'm ready to find Ramon's boss a date—maybe he'll hook up and change his schedule. And while they're at it they can change Ramon's schedule... Didn't you also have an "available" friend? Listen, invite her to the cinema next time, and I'll tell Ramon to bring his boss and the five of us will go to the movies and see what happens... Haha...

And what's more, lately his phone never stops ringing, man... Thankfully he puts it on silent when he gets home, but even so, we're eating and you hear the buzz of the alarm, "bzzzzzz, bzzzzz..." And on the weekend, you wouldn't believe ... Honestly, it's no wonder poor Ramon is tired and anxious—this is no way to live...

Well, let's talk next week; we'll see if this husband of mine comes back to life a little and we can meet.

OK?

Hugs!!!

Maria

Subject: This week's bad too...
Date: 22 June 2010, 09:34:15 + 0100
From: Maria <marieta@mail.com>
To: Juan <juanitu@mail.com>

Hi Juan!!!

In case I don't get hold of you two days from now, I wanted to send my wishes now...

HAPPY NAME DAY! I hope you have a wonderful Saint John's Eve and an even happier Saint John's Day!. Don't overdo it with the cake and the cava, and be careful with the fireworks lest there be an accident...

We're going to spend Saint John's Eve at home. Well, me the whole night and Ramon part of it—he has to work late on the 23rd. And he doesn't get a long weekend; can you believe it? He has to go back to work on Friday and on Saturday morning. They did at least give him the 24th off—if they hadn't it would be enough to file a complaint...

Since we can't go anywhere I'm going to take the opportunity to sort the closets—I've had it in mind for a while, but since I've been overwhelmed the last few weeks with the damn trip and all, I still have a lot of stuff to pick up, clean up and pack up. It seems unreal how things accumulate over the years, man...

I'm not suggesting meeting up because I know myself and when I get into "housewife mode" I get excited and end up not having enough hours in the day...

One thing: do you remember the mole on my shoulder? I think it was the last time we saw each other (or maybe the time before that, but anyway, it was fairly recently) that I mentioned that the mole on my shoulder was getting bigger. Well, now I have a visit scheduled with the dermatologist to have a look at it, for the first week of July.

Now that Ramon isn't feeling well maybe I'm more scared of getting sick than usual. Can you imagine both of us sick at once? We would die! It's plain that I take care of Ramon, and when he's sick I make sure to prepare the fish he likes, fix the soup he feels like having, give him his medication—well, the usual stuff.

Oh, but when it's me that doesn't feel well, poor Ramon—he can't find anything, he doesn't know where anything is, as if he didn't live here! So, you know, I haven't been sick many times, and I am easily contented, but when I mentioned the freckle and stuff he was insistent that I make an appointment right away... And this is from a man who has seemed like a soul in purgatory for days... But he says it's not the same and that I have to take care of myself, that I am what keeps this house together and all... He's so good...

And that's it; I listened to him and have an appointment now. Now, let's see if he can take the day off to come with me—I don't want to go alone...

I'll let you go now; I have a pile of things to do. It doesn't seem possible, man: you do things at home and it's like they come undone themselves...

Speak to you soon!, Maria

Subject: What are you doing tomorrow afternoon?
Date: 2 July 2010, 16:04:10 + 0100
From: Maria <marieta@mail.com>
To: Juan <juanitu@mail.com>

Hey Juan!!

What are you doing tomorrow afternoon? I have my dermatologist appointment to go to and Ramon has just now told me he can't come with me... What a hassle!

I wanted to ask you if you could accompany me. You know how very faint of heart I am and how I hate, HATE, to go to the doctor alone... If you can't, no worries—I can call a taxi; lately it's as if I have a subscription because I've had to call them more often than I would have liked. It's honestly very lucky that Ramon is friends with the guy from the taxi company because they always have one ready for me and they take me, wait for me and bring me home. Like a queen!

See, a while back I was thinking about whether or not I should get my driver's license, but since Ramon has always taken me everywhere and I go everywhere around town on foot, shop locally, etc., the truth is that for the rare occasion that I need to go somewhere alone it wasn't worth it.

Ramon made a quick tally and it worked out better for me to pay the taxis when need be than to have a car and all. And I wouldn't need to worry about parking. And what can I say, he's right...

All of that to ask you if you can come with me. Let me know as soon as possible, please.

Thanks! M.

Subject: Ramon's in the hospital
Date: 5 July 2010, 09:39:15 + 0100
From: Maria <marieta@mail.com>
To: Juan <juanitu@mail.com>

Juan,

Ramon is in hospital. As soon as he came home on Saturday, he didn't even have lunch or anything and went to lie down in bed. In the evening he started to say he couldn't breathe, and even though he didn't want me to, I called an ambulance.

It looks like it may have been a small heart attack, but it's nothing to joke about and they have admitted him.

I came home for a bit to get clothes and I'm going back to the hospital.

I'll call you when I can; over there I have my cell phone turned off.

Maria

Subject: Everything is OK
Date: 6 July 2010, 10:05:22 + 0100
From: Maria <marieta@mail.com>
To: Juan <juanitu@mail.com>

Juan,

I'm a bit calmer writing now... As they said, it looks like it was a very mild heart attack, but everything is under control.

If nothing else happens they'll send us home before the weekend.

Sorry for not calling; I'm writing to you making use of having come home to bring the dirty clothes and turn off Ramon's phone—the poor man is worried because he says that it will bug me if it's ringing all the time...

I tried to see if I could do it since it's one of those touchscreen ones, and I think I put it on silent but didn't turn it off... I'll try again later.

I'm going back to the hospital now and I'll keep you up to speed.

Maria

Subject: Everything OK
Date: 8 July 2010, 14:45:17 + 0100
From: Maria <marieta@mail.com>
To: Juan <juanitu@mail.com>

Juan,

My battery died. All these days I've forgotten to charge my phone, and just when you called this morning it died completely. I'm sorry...

I came home for a minute to get the charger and pick up something to read.

The doctor's say Ramon is better and that everything is going as planned. Poor thing, he's been in an awful way all these days there; he hardly eats anything and barely gets any rest.

I'll call you in a couple of hours when the doctor comes by; maybe I'll be able to tell you we're on our way home...

Speak to you in a bit,

Maria

SMS

Date: 9 July 2010, 12:13:17 + 0100

From: Maria <629XXXXXX>

To: Juan <639XXXXXX>

RAMON IS DEAD. PLEASE COME TO HOSPITAL.

M.

Subject:
Date: 16 July 2010, 05:23:18 + 0100
From: Maria <marieta@mail.com>
To: Juan <juanitu@mail.com>

Ramon has been gone for a week

I don't know what to do

I don't know what I'm doing

I can't sleep, but I want to sleep, and wake up and for all of this to have been a bad dream

This can't be, it can't be, it can't be

Juan, I can't cry anymore, and it's the only thing I feel like doing

Ramon, where are you?

Ramon, Ramon, Ramon

I need this to be over now and for Ramon to come back, please, please, please

Subject:
Date: 19 July 2010, 03:58:43 + 0100
From: Maria <marieta@mail.com>
To: Juan <juanitu@mail.com>

Juan,

With little sleep in me, with the tears I can't get out of my eyes, with a strange mix of sadness, impotence and incredulity that hasn't left me for the last 10 days, which have seemed an eternity, going back and forth to the telephone constantly because I hope someone will call at some point, or that Ramon will call me and I'll wake up.

I am infinitely grateful for your attention.

I am infinitely grateful that you accompanied me while they cremated Ramon.

I am infinitely grateful that you accompanied me home with his ashes.

It's all I have left of him.

I put them on the night table and I fall asleep touching the urn. I don't have anything else.

You've called me a bunch of times and I've only picked up sometimes. And I wouldn't want to be rude to you, but it's hard for me to talk to anyone. Even to you.

I know I can count on you. I have always known this. But I don't have the strength to talk.

I trust that you understand and forgive me.

Excuse me because maybe I'm writing in a rush, but the tears come to my eyes when I think about it, when I breathe.

I can't find the words to write everything that I feel—I would fill full screens with "IT CAN'T BE, IT CAN'T BE, IT CAN'T BE, IT CAN'T BE," but I'm afraid that wouldn't change anything.

These days have been different; there are things in my life that will never, EVER, be the same again. Nothing will ever be the same again.

What will I do with my life?

What will I do without Ramon?

It hurts to write his name, but it's what comes to mind and mouth constantly.

His name

I suppose it will be inevitable for me to have to learn to live with this tightness in my chest, with this weight that smothers me, with what I have now and don't want.

I don't know if I'll be able to. I don't know if I'll want to. I don't know anything.

I just looked at my phone in case Ramon had called

And he can't call me, huh? But I want him to call me

I don't know what I want. But I don't want what I have now. Not this.

M.

Subject:
Date: 23 July 2010, 19:18:02 + 0100
From: Maria <marieta@mail.com>
To: Juan <juanitu@mail.com>

Some of the girls from work came to see me today. They were very sweet.

They offered to take care of the paperwork so I wouldn't have to go back to work right now, and I accepted.

I wouldn't be able to bear everyone looking at me and asking.

Not yet.

I can't stop thinking about what has happened. I still don't understand it. Everything was fine, everything was under control; we were about to come home.

I looked at the paperwork they gave me. I had to look at it to give it to the girls from work.

Ictus. I had never paid attention to that word before, until now.

I have jumbled memories from the last days.

The hardest part was signing the organ bank documents. Now someone will have his eyes and maybe his heart and I don't know which other parts. They told me that I will never know who has them, but that I should feel pleased to know that thanks to Ramon someone will be able to have a more decent life.

It is unfair that someone needs someone else to live. It is unfair that I don't have Ramon. I need him to live

The girls from work said that I need to find something positive in all of this. I don't know what they were thinking.

There is NOTHING positive about this. NOTHING

I am very alone. I don't want to be alone. I have never wanted to be.

I will be alone, so alone, forever.

M.

Subject:
Date: 24 July 2010, 06:23:02 + 0100
From: Maria <marieta@mail.com>
To: Juan <juanitu@mail.com>

Today I woke up needing to write you.

I have been running it over and over in my head for days. I can't do anything else.

I can't get the last few days out of my head. But at the same time, scenes from my life come to mind. Of my life with Ramon.

I never met my father, and I suppose that's why I've never missed him. And my only sister left home very young, when I was 10 years old, and it was always as if I were an only child, with my Mom.

I had a normal childhood and my youth was also very normal. My Mom and me.

When I met Ramon, it made my Mom very happy. She liked him so much, from the first day...

And we were about to get married when Mom told us that she was ill. She didn't want us to change anything at all. Everything was to be done as we had planned.

And Ramon was so sensitive—he let me change what I wanted for the day to be perfect, even though Mom was sick.

He was so wonderful... And he made me feel so loved and so good...

When Mom died, Ramon helped me so much, was so there for me, gave me so much support that I knew I wasn't alone.

My sister, who had barely made an appearance over the years Mom was sick, not even when she was dying, told us after Mom was buried that she was moving into the house. And she was lucky that Ramon convinced me, because at that moment I would have kicked her out if I could have... Well, we were both lucky, because he helped us to bridge the gap between us.

It was Ramon who found a way for us to sit down and talk. We had always been apart, and we were two strangers. Sisters, but we didn't know each other at all.

Her story comes to mind, her falling out with Mom—they were very different, and she, my sister, was a free spirit. She was taken in by the lights and colors of the show world. I found out then that she was a "vedette." At that time, I didn't know what "vedettes" did, but I didn't imagine a life as sad as the one she told me about.

An argument between a "conventional" mother and her daughter, young and overenergetic, too proud, ended up separating the two of them. And Mom was proud too. She waited for her to come back saying she'd been wrong. She had let her make her mistakes. And my sister didn't come back so as not to say Mom had been right. And she lived a very lonely life all these years.

My mom almost never spoke about my sister to me. Only on her name day and her birthday would she say, "Today is your sister's name day." She never said "my daughter's."

She stayed in Mom's house and told me not to worry, that she wouldn't be there forever.

And in the end she did stay forever, but "forever" was just under two years. I guess that's what she wanted to tell me.

When my sister died, it didn't feel the same as when Mom died. I felt sorry, and the life the two of us had missed out on made me sad, but I was with Ramon then and I felt sufficiently comforted and supported. She was the one who had died alone, and that is what grieved me the most. And Ramon helped me so much in putting everything in order. Papers, money, graves, wills, inheritance etc. If it hadn't been for him, I don't know what I would have done all alone, losing everything in two years.

And I never felt alone because I had him. And now... Now I am alone. Completely alone. And I miss my Mom and my sister. I had hardly missed them these years, but now I do.

And I needed to tell you all of this. But not on the phone or speaking to you. I couldn't have.

I read what I've written you and I see that I have given a summary of my life. There isn't much to the story of my life. And now I have even less.

That's what I wanted to tell you.

Maria

Subject:
Date: 25 July 2010, 06:23:02 + 0100
From: Maria <marieta@mail.com>
To: Juan <juanitu@mail.com>

Yesterday I sent you a rather long email. I really needed to let it all out.

And I'd like to be able to do more of that, but I only have one subject: Ramon.

And I don't want to bore you, because then I won't have anyone to write.

I'm just writing to you today to tell you that I am calm.

I was looking at photographs. All day long. I have so many memories of happiness...

Some, the pictures from the first few years, are becoming discolored, but when I look at them the moment when they were taken comes to me, and if I close my eyes I remember the voices and the smells.

The last ones I looked at on the computer—I haven't had a chance to take them to be printed yet. And now I won't, because I don't have anyone to share them with.

I was running my fingers over the first pictures I have with Ramon, at Colònia Güell. We hadn't been there in a while now, and he'd said we'd go for our anniversary in October.

I won't be going now. I don't want to go there alone; I won't go.

And I was looking at the photos from our wedding, and I saw how Mom was looking at us. Happy but with a sorrow in her eyes she couldn't hide. And now, when I look at myself in the mirror, I look like her... Sad.

And I was looking at the photos from my sister's last year, before she'd said she didn't want any more photos taken because her illness was very apparent.

And Ramon is hardly ever in those photos because he was the one taking them.

And now I'm sorry I didn't take more pictures of him.

I looked at pictures, I cried, I wiped the tears away and I looked at photos again. And I started crying again.

I don't want to look at any more photos now.

I guess it's time to start with the music now. There's so much to choose from, so many songs and melodies that remind me of him. So many moments with "our song"...

And I think of that September in 1979 when I met him... And I have never written anything about that, and I don't know if I'll be able to...

I'll try...

He had gone to a student demonstration with some friends. He wasn't a political extremist or anything, but at the time he thought it was something he had to do. And he hid from the police in our doorway.

I wanted to go out and see what was going on, and when I opened the door he snuck into our house.

I remember that the first thing he pulled out was his ID card so we would see his name and that he was good people." And I asked him if the thing about "good people" was written before or after "profession."

And he stared at the ID card as if he wanted to see where it was, before or after.

I laughed so hard at his innocence in that nervous moment, and we let him stay.

When he left a few hours later, he had already asked Mom if he could call and invite me to the cinema.

He never went to another demonstration.

And that's how I met him, without leaving home. That October afternoon fortune came looking for me. And one year later, also in October, we got married.

And this October we won't be able to celebrate our anniversary; we won't be able to go to Colònia Güell or anywhere.

Destiny, which brought him to me, has come now to take him away from me...

I can't write anymore. Not today...

Maria

Subject:
Date: 28 July 2010, 10:13:32 + 0100
From: Maria <marieta@mail.com>
To: Juan <juanitu@mail.com>

Looking at photos and keepsakes, I found one from when we met.

The truth is that I hadn't thought about it again. How long have we known each other? How did we meet?

I was looking at the pictures from our silver anniversary— Ramon wanted us to celebrate at the same chapel where we had gotten married 25 years earlier. And you're there, with your bow tie and keyboard.

On that occasion it was only family from his side, for the ceremony, and there weren't many of them either... His brother and his wife and boys were there, with faces of boredom they couldn't conceal. And there were two of his friends from work with their wives.

Ramon's brother made a derisive comment because there weren't even a dozen of us.

And then Ramon says to me, "I'm going to invite that guy with the keyboard and then there will be 12 of us".

Life is strange...

I might still have to thank Ramon's brother for his impertinence one day; because that is how we met you and now I have someone.

Because they only paid attention to me on the day of the burial, in front of people—you saw it—but that was it. Afterwards they called once to offer to look at Ramon's papers "so I wouldn't miss anything". What could I miss? What have they got to do with it?

I told them we could talk in September, that I didn't feel like it now.

And it's true that I don't feel like it.

This year makes 30 years since we got married. We didn't have to do anything special. He and I. But now I'll have to do it on my own.

Everything I think about, everything I do ends up leading me to the reality and evidence that I don't have him anymore, he is not with me anymore.

I am left all alone. It's terrible, Juan.

Maria

Subject:
Date: 31 July 2010, 07:37:30 + 0100
From: Maria <marieta@mail.com>
To: Juan <juanitu@mail.com>

Juan,

I feel panicky this August. We had planned on a very different holiday month.

We wanted to go to Rome. Now we will never go. Ramon and I.

One of the girls from work invited me to go with her to the village where her parents live. Just for two weeks; that's fine with me.

Far enough from home not to hear the silence that surrounds me. Far enough not to notice the smell of his absence. Far.

I am sure I will go, because I need to breathe and I am almost suffocating.

How is it possible? I have been so happy between these walls and now they are like a prison...

All of this is unreal.

I had to find a lawyer because we hadn't made a will, and since we didn't have any children—I don't know what they were telling me about the Catalan system and usufruct and inheritance...

I don't feel up to doing any of that.

A girl from work gave me the name of a lawyer and I asked him to take care of everything. He was talking to me about some powers of attorney to save me hassle.

Frankly, I will be very appreciative.

How could Ramon have done this? How? I still find myself saying to myself, "It can't be"...

I think I will go with the girl from work. I've discovered that there are really great people around me.

I also know you're there—you've always been there—but I meant to say that I have found other people.

Later I'm going to the hairdresser to get a bit done to my hair. I'm not going to get it cut but I should get it dyed.

And I'll do it the same as usual; Ramon didn't like for me to wear it unkempt and always encouraged me to cover the gray with dye.

He said that the gray didn't do me justice.

Always so sweet.

I'll have my phone on me these days.

M.

Subject:
Date: 16 August 2010, 05:05:22 + 0100
From: Maria <marieta@mail.com>
To: Juan <juanitu@mail.com>

Juan,

I appreciate you calling me these days while I was away.

These two weeks have been good. There were a lot of people at my coworker's house, and lots of things to do, and everyone has been very nice.

It's not that I stopped thinking about Ramon, because I can't, but I was able to disconnect at some point.

Just at some point, because Ramon is on my mind all the time. He can't think I don't love him.

It's funny... There are times when his face gets blurry if I think about it a lot. But no, I look at a picture and I see everything and I remember everything. His voice, his smell, the way he walked...

How could this have happened, Juan?

I wanted to tell you that I don't want to stay at home for what's left of August.

I'm going to L'Estartit. I have to see if I can go there without him. I have to do it. Every summer we spent a week there on holiday and this year I want to do it too.

I told my coworker and she helped me find buses from Barcelona that leave you in the town center. I haven't made any reservations.

If they don't have any vacancies where we always went I'll catch the last bus back and be done with it.

But I want to try it.

Thanks for always being there on the other side.

M.

Subject: I'm going back to work tomorrow
Date: 29 August 2010, 22:25:46 + 0100
From: Maria <marieta@mail.com>
To: Juan <juanitu@mail.com>

Hi Juan

This week has been terrible.

I walked along the beach without him. I walked along the promenade in the evening without him. I stayed in front of the Medes Islands for hours hoping that at some moment he would come up behind me, cover my eyes and ask, "Who am I?"

But he didn't come. I'm starting to see that he's never coming again. And I don't believe it, yet.

I'm going back to work tomorrow.

Tomorrow afternoon I'll call you or write. I'll tell you how it went.

I'm taking the opportunity to go back to work these first few days before September when there aren't many people there.

And when I get home I won't be waiting for anyone. And no one will be waiting for me…

Talk to you tomorrow.

M.

Subject: Ramon's name day
Date: 31 August 2010, 16:05:36 + 0100
From: Maria <marieta@mail.com>
To: Juan <juanitu@mail.com>

Juan,

Today is Ramon's name day.

I miss him so much—so much.

Other years we joined the pilgrimage up to the shrine for the Saint's feast, but this year we won't be going.

Call me if you can.

M.

Subject: First week
Date: 3 September 2010, 15:55:40 + 0100
From: Maria <marieta@mail.com>
To: Juan <juanitu@mail.com>

Hey Juan

I've made it through the first week of work.

The first two days were horrible because the few people there were fussing over me and I wanted to be alone. But I didn't say anything. The other days were also horrible because everyone was coming back happy from vacation.

But not me. I'm not coming back from vacation nor am I happy. And maybe I would have liked not to return from anywhere.

I met the coworker who wasn't able to go to Rome. We've kept each other company these days. Both of us are alone. At least she knows her husband is alive and can hope he'll come back to her. This isn't a comfort to her, but I would rather Ramon was with another woman and alive.

Ramon will never come back.

She told me that hers won't come back either; the woman he's with now is very young and her husband will have kids and be young. And she couldn't have children anymore now.

I told her that we, Ramon and I, never needed them. We didn't have them, but we didn't worry about it. We always had each other. We always had...

My coworker, from what she told me, couldn't have children (she couldn't), and she suspects that that is why her husband went looking for another woman. We stopped talking because we started to cry and it can't be.

The lawyer called me. I get lost in his language. He told me not to worry; he will let me know if there's anything new. And he told me not to be concerned, that no one will kick me out of my house. I was on the verge of saying something fresh but I didn't feel like arguing. If he says that everything "looks good" for now, I'll trust him...

This week I have slept regularly—few hours, but every day, every night, and I was thankful.

One of the girls at work offered to help me gather up Ramon's things and I was shocked... Why would I want to gather anything up? Everything is as he left it.

All I did was to wash the dirty laundry in the basket to leave it folded in its place. But what was in the closets is exactly as it was.

Why should I tidy it up?

She says that I need to do it and start to "turn the page" and start a new chapter.

But I don't want to turn the page.

I want to read all the pages that have been written.

Because I will never write them again.

Anyway, I just wanted to tell you that.

We'll be in touch.

Subject: First *Diada*
Date: 12 September 2010, 08:20:32 + 0100
From: Maria <marieta@mail.com>
To: Juan <juanitu@mail.com>

Hey Juan

Yesterday was the *Diada* (Catalonia's national feast). Yesterday made 2 months since we buried Ramon.

There is something that reminds me of him every day that passes. Every hour, every minute, there are little things that bring him to me.

And I realize that he is no longer with me.

I didn't leave the house, not even to go to the floral tribute. Too many people, too many acquaintances, too many... And I still don't have the heart to face up to so much reality...

He really loved to go there. And he sang the song of the Catalan national flag in his deep, imposing voice, and hearing him people would turn to see who was singing.

When I heard the song today while the flag was being hoisted, I closed my eyes and listened for his voice but it wasn't there. And my eyes flooded with tears.

I turned the sound off then and just left the image. No voices, in silence.

Like my life has been the last two months: in silence.

See? I'm crying again. It's all still too recent for me. Or it will always be recent for me. I don't know. But I feel like crying today, here, in the shelter of my home, and I'm crying.

I don't cry at work. Only the first day. But I managed not to cry in front of anyone; I don't want anyone to pity me. The pity is mine; it's for myself. The world can have its own pity. This is mine.

I was thinking this week that the girls from work are right about "turning the page." Not entirely, but one page, just one.

The matter of the closets, for example. If I clean them out, I can give all the clothes that can be used to the nursing home and someone will be able to benefit from them.

And yesterday afternoon I started with the closets.

The first door I opened gave me a jolt. As I opened it, his smell hit me, and it gripped me so tightly I almost fell over. I had to sit down for a while and breathe deeply. And I cried. A lot.

I spent a long while running my hand over his suits. Without taking them down...

It was very hard to decide which ones to keep and which ones to let go...

I guess I'll have to go through them several times because I only took out a fourth of what's there and the rest is still in the closet (everything has so many memories attached...).

I cleaned out the pockets of the ones I took out and put them, neatly folded, in a bag.

Before I realized it, it had almost gotten dark.

And I opened a second door, shirts, and the same thing happened, and this time I anticipated it. I set aside a few of those too. I folded them carefully and put them in the bag as well.

When I finished it was very late. I was exhausted and even more so with how hot it's been these last few days.

Now I've just gotten up and I'll need to do the rest of the closet, the drawers and shoes. I went to bed with my hair wet from the shower last night, and now I have a headache. Just what I needed on top of everything.

This is hard, Juan. Very hard.

I just wanted to tell you.

Maria

Subject: Parcels
Date: 13 September 2010, 23:05:30 + 0100
From: Maria <marieta@mail.com>
To: Juan <juanitu@mail.com>

Juan,

I've started to pack up clothes.

Some parcels, or rather bags, are going to the nursing home. Some other parcels will go up to the attic because I don't want to get rid of everything of Ramon's.

I bought plastic bags that connect to the vacuum cleaner to remove the air and make compact parcels of clothing.

I made three parcels of suits, all of them nicely packed.

I made one parcel of long-sleeved and short-sleeved shirts and another with jerseys and summer polo shirts.

And I made another parcel with sportswear and underwear.

I've run out of bags and I'll have to go get a couple more to pack up the shoes and trainers.

When I unpacked his squash bag I started crying. I've watched him take the clean clothes out of it so many times lately.

And they hadn't been touched this time either. And I put the clothes away just as they were.

I put everything I took out of the pockets and the gym bag in a drawer. There are a lot of empty spaces now, and the room seems to echo with all this space...

I'll have to look at the paperwork at some point. But not this week. Saturday we'll see.

I'm going to bring the bags to the nursing home in the afternoons. That way they'll have everything before it gets chilly.

I'll also have to look at his phone.

I left it plugged in on silent when Ramon was in the hospital.

Good thing I didn't turn it off like he had asked me to because I wouldn't have known how to turn it on and when I have a look at it I'll be able to respond if someone's tried to reach him.

And I'm sure there are messages because there's a little light blinking. I didn't touch the telephone because that way it's like it always was when he had it plugged in, with the little light blinking. And if I do something and that light goes out I'll be even more alone and wouldn't want that.

But I won't be looking at it this week. Saturday I'll get started on the paperwork and then the phone.

It's gotten really late, so I'm going to bed. I'm so tired I'm sure I'll sleep well tonight.

Speak to you soon.

Maria

Subject: More parcels
Date: 17 September 2010, 22:12:05 + 0100
From: Maria <marieta@mail.com>
To: Juan <juanitu@mail.com>

Juan,

I took the bags to the nursing home. I took them on different days because there was so much stuff: suits, jerseys, shirts, shoes, underwear (I only took what was new; what he had used I left at home).

I was left with a strange feeling after I'd left all of it at the reception desk.

As if I was getting rid of a part of me.

Now I have to take up to the attic all the parcels I made of clothes I don't want to give away.

For now I want them with me.

And I left a few changes of clothes and everything in the closet. Just in case.

I figure you'll say that it makes no sense, but I feel much better if I see some of his things in the closets.

My life is already empty enough to have empty closets too.

I took some time to sort through his personal stuff and then brought some things of aftershave, shaving cream and new razors to the nursing home.

I even made a bag of bath towels, the ones he took to squash, and one of bathrobes he had "just in case."

I left the other bathrobe in the bathroom, next to mine.

Anyway, I finished the week exhausted.

And tomorrow, I said that I would set about looking at the paperwork, receipts and slips; I pulled out a stack of VISA payment slips—he was the one who checked them before throwing them away and now I'll have to do it. I went to the bank yesterday to ask for online access because he did all of that until now but at some point I'll have to start doing it.

I made use of the visit to open a new account yesterday, in just my name, and I'll start transferring the money from our joint accounts over to this one because the lawyer told me I should.

It looks like Ramon's brother was checking to see if he has a legal right to anything since we had never made a will. I had a feeling he would do that. And I'm sure he's "not doing it for himself; he's doing it for the boys," as he always says. He never does anything for himself, he always does it for the boys, but he's the one who does it.

It's the lawyer who's checking over everything. The apartment belonged to both of them (Ramon and his brother) and it looks like they do have a right to a part of it, but they can't kick me out or make me sell it. I'll explain it better later, but it seems I have usufruct rights throughout my lifetime.

Ramon always looked out for his nephews, when they were studying, when they said they wanted to get married and when they had their kids. And I always found them a bit opportunistic but Ramon didn't want to see it that way.

And I figured they would jump on it to see "what they could get"—it was a matter of time.

But I didn't think it would be so soon. I thought they would wait a bit longer.

Well, the lawyer will be in charge of it. And I'll do what I have to do. And I'll give them whatever's theirs, but when the time comes.

Tomorrow I'll start looking at paperwork.

And the phone... that is going to be some work... I found the instructions and I'm reading them so I don't do anything wrong or turn it off.

We'll be in touch.

Maria

Núria Salán Ballesteros

Subject: Papers and receipts
Date: 18 September 2010, 22:55:36 + 0100
From: Maria <marieta@mail.com>
To: Juan <juanitu@mail.com>

Juan,

I didn't think this would affect me so much.

I cleaned out all of the papers, parking receipts he'd left in his pockets, gas receipts, notes that mean nothing to me...

I made piles and put them in chronological order.

There's a parking lot he seems to have liked a lot because it's the only one there are receipts from.

But when I looked at the card payments online there weren't any for parking. Then I noticed that the card number is not one of "ours."

I looked in his wallet. There were more slips of paper and receipts, and when I looked at the cards I found one that's not one of the "home" ones.

I guess it's from work because it's the one he used to pay for parking and all of the receipts are from Fridays and Saturdays, which is why I figure it's for work stuff.

He must have forgotten to tell me that they were meeting outside the office some days—the Swedes do that...

And I found a receipt from a jewelry store.

That was my discovery.

I burst into tears because that means I had a gift coming and he wasn't able to give it to me. His last gift.

I'd like to go and get it next week, but I don't want to go alone. Would you please come with me?

I feel a mix of sorrow, impatience, elation, excitement and fear.

I've never gone to get anything for myself; it was always he who surprised me. And he always made just the right choice. I don't know how I'll manage to do so many things without him.

I don't know if I'll manage...

Juan, all of this is so hard...

I went to the hairdresser's this afternoon. They asked me if I wanted to cut my hair and I said no, I want to leave it long like this, the way Ramon liked it.

Please call me Monday so we can make plans.

Maria

Subject:
Date: 22 September 2010, 16:15:01 + 0100
From: Maria <marieta@mail.com>
To: Juan <juanitu@mail.com>

I don't know where to start

I don't know what to say

Juan, I'm shattered...

I was not expecting this

I don't know how to handle it...

I can't...

M

Subject:
Date: 24 September 2010, 19:25:31 + 0100
From: Maria <marieta@mail.com>
To: Juan <juanitu@mail.com>

I looked at the bank accounts again.

I started to look in his phone.

I must be mistaken. It can't be.

It can't be

IT CAN'T BE!

I don't know how to explain the transfers into an account that's in his name only. At the bank they told me that the card is linked to this account.

But they can't tell me anything because my name's not on the account. I'll never have the right to know because I'm not his heir.

I'm only his widow.

That's all.

And luckily they were willing to tell me the card went with the account—they didn't have to tell me, but we've been with this bank for many years.

My whole life with Ramon.

My whole life.

It's not about the money; it's about why he hadn't told me he had this account.

And he used that card to pay for the thing from the jewelry store.

And parking.

There were a lot of calls from clients on Ramon's phone—I listened to the voicemail and the messages were from work. I left those calls aside.

But the other calls, the ones made from the same number, from "R," there are no voicemails from them.

Only text messages.

"I'm waiting for you"

"Are you coming today?"

"Everything is ready"

"Don't be long"

"Kisses"

"I love you"

Who the hell was saying this to Ramon?

And the texts he was sending?

It can't be.

It can't be anything else.

"I miss you"

"I can stay today"

"See you soon"

"Very soon"

"I love you"

IT CAN'T BE!

Who is "R"?

And it can't be one of his coworkers because he wouldn't buy a heart with "R and R" for any of them.

Ramon and "R."

Who the hell is "R"????

Juan, I'm very nervous

Subject:
Date: 26 September 2010, 12:30:11 + 0100
From: Maria <marieta@mail.com>
To: Juan <juanitu@mail.com>

I'm mortified

And I am enraged

And I don't know to handle it all.

I didn't think there could be anything worse than having lost Ramon. And I was wrong. This is much worse.

I'm turning a lot of things over in my head, Juan.

So many Fridays working. So many Saturday mornings.

So many days of squash—he would tell me he was going to squash and then he has a parking receipt from the same place as ever.

And now I understand why he encouraged me to go to Rome...

The parking from that weekend is for having spent every day there, at "R"'s house.

I'm going crazy

Christ, Juan, this should not have happened...

How did I get here? How could I not have noticed anything? How could I have been so thick?

Everything is a shambles, Juan, everything.

What have I left now? I HAVE NOTHING LEFT!

What will I do now, Juan? What will I do?

I am very lonely and very sad. And hurt

I feel hollow inside

I thought of the destruction of tropical hurricanes shaking everything and destroying structures people thought solid.

This has been a hurricane. But only for me.

And now what?

Subject: I didn't go to work
Date: 27 September 2010, 11:10:07 + 0100
From: Maria <marieta@mail.com>
To: Juan <juanitu@mail.com>

Juan,

I took this week off work.

I can't think about anything.

My head is swimming with things.

My house is full of parcels of Ramon's things.

I haven't finished gathering them up and this has made me want to search through everything that's left.

I haven't found anything else. The parking receipts, the receipt from the jewelry store and the messages on his phone.

Such little things and how badly they've hurt me.

I have to think about what to do with all of this.

I listened to the voicemail you left me. I don't feel like going out. Thank you so much, but I don't feel like it.

Another week, Juan, please.

M.

Subject:
Date: 28 September 2010, 11:10:07 + 0100
From: Maria <marieta@mail.com>
To: Juan <juanitu@mail.com>

I showed up to Ramon's work today.

I talked with his boss, the Swede. That was true if nothing else was.

He was very nice. Very considerate.

I guess he doesn't know anything about Ramon and "R," but I didn't bring it up.

I still have dignity.

I told him I had Ramon's work phone with the calls from clients. He said that it was a personal phone and that almost all of the clients had already called after not receiving a response.

It looks like I shouldn't worry about it. As much as he worried about "work"...

I told him if any of Ramon's coworkers wanted anything of his they should let me know because I was planning to get rid of a lot of personal stuff.

As you might have imagined, no one asked for the squash set.

I suspect that he had never played with people from work...

He told me that their legal services team was still working on the papers for death benefits and so on. And that if I wanted to I could pick up Ramon's personal stuff—they'd put it in a box.

They're going to call me and I'll probably go back there in a couple of days.

I did what I had to do, and admittedly I hoped to run into someone who looked like "R."

Sometimes I am very simple.

The only people that came to say hello to me were his two coworkers who were at our silver anniversary and who were also at the burial, and two men I don't remember having ever seen.

No women came to say anything to me.

Actually, there are very few there, but I thought one of them would come up to me. None did.

And then, when I was just about to leave, it occurred to me...

I asked to go to the restroom and when I was inside I looked for "R"'s number, I put it in my phone, I opened the door to the restroom... And I called.

A phone rang out in the room and gave me a start. I hung up. And I left in a hurry.

Afterwards, when I had already left the building and was going to look for a taxi, "R" called my cell phone.

I didn't know what to do, whether to answer it or not.

I picked up and heard a very pleasant female voice asking who I was, saying she'd gotten a call from me.

Suddenly, I don't know how, I said that I didn't know who I was speaking with, that this was Maria, and she said, "This is Rose..."

Then I caught my breath and said: "Hello Rose. This is Maria, Ramon's wife."

And she hung up. I don't know what her face looks like, but she has a name: Rose

R and R

Ramon and Rose. Rose and Ramon. I am hurting myself.

I went back to Ramon's office and sat on a bench outside, watching the door.

A lot of people came out but I didn't recognize any of their faces or features. I saw the women that had been in the main room come out, and I know that she is one of them but I don't know which one.

I know that this is unhealthy but I need to do it.

I have never done anything alone in my life; I think this is the only time I have ever had the initiative to do something...

And look what has led me to do it...

Everything is a mess...

M.

Subject:
Date: 1 October 2010, 23:22:09 + 0100
From: Maria <marieta@mail.com>
To: Juan <juanitu@mail.com>

Ramon's boss called me yesterday to tell me I could go pick up his things whenever I liked. I told him I would go today and I did.

They gave me a box with his initials. That's all. R.M.P. No date or anything.

A chill came over me.

Ramon's coworkers offered to bring me home but I told them I had a taxi outside. It wasn't true, but I wasn't in the mood for uncomfortable silences.

Another parcel of Ramon's. They put it in a cart for me and I told them I would bring it down and didn't want to disturb them.

I asked to go to the restroom, and I told them that I knew where it was.

On my way, I looked around for a face I didn't recognize. I saw a man at one end of the room, and as I was going to the restroom I asked him if he could please tell me which was Rose's desk...

And he indicated one towards the center of the room where the telephone had rung the other day.

And there was "R." I stood frozen there in the middle, looking at the nape of a woman's neck, a woman without a face, but I was taken aback when I saw that she has hair so short I could have thought she were a man if it weren't for her patterned blouse.

That short, short hair…

And she turned around. And I saw her face. For a couple of seconds we looked at each other. And she saw me.

I went in the bathroom and I was nauseous.

I am not that strong, Juan. I'm not.

I calmed myself down and walked out, not knowing how to handle it… but she wasn't there.

Now I know what "R"'s face looks like.

I came home and got into bed. I think I had a fever. I slept fitfully all afternoon.

I didn't want to think about it but I couldn't get away from the images that came to mind.

Ramon and her. Ramon and Rose.

With such short hair.

This sucks, Juan

M.

Subject:
Date: 3 October 2010, 22:10:34 + 0100
From: Maria <marieta@mail.com>
To: Juan <juanitu@mail.com>

I left home this weekend.

Saturday morning I put a change of clothes in a bag and went to the station.

I got a ticket to the end of the line.

I looked for a hotel and spent the weekend in Manresa.

I didn't do anything. I just walked down different streets seeing different faces.

I wanted faces and places that didn't remind me of Ramon.

I got some rest.

I got back a couple of hours ago. I ran a bath and stayed in it until the water got cool.

I dried my hair—I've gone to bed with wet hair and then I get a headache.

My heartache is enough for me.

I'll give you a call this week.

M.

Subject:
Date: 13 October 2010, 15:15:14 + 0100
From: Maria <marieta@mail.com>
To: Juan <juanitu@mail.com>

Juan,

You're going to say it's foolish, but it's too late because I've already done it.

I called one of Ramon's coworkers.

I'm meeting him this afternoon.

I can't live with the things I imagine. Whatever it is, I want to know.

M.

Subject:
Date: 15 October 2010, 16:19:30 + 0100
From: Maria <marieta@mail.com>
To: Juan <juanitu@mail.com>

I needed a day to take it all in.

I met up with Ramon's coworker. He knew about the thing with Rose. Ramon had told him. It looks like it's been about two years since "this story" started.

Rose had a partner and they only saw each other from time to time. But a few months ago, she split up with him and was left single. Ramon then ran after her. And they started to see each other very often, Fridays, weekends.

He told me that he was very sorry but he expected it would end one day or another.

What he didn't tell me is which side he thought it would end on. Rose's or mine.

And when I asked him, he lowered his head.

I would never have imagined I'd have the nerve to do what I did.

Never.

I'm discovering myself.

I don't know if I like me.

M.

Subject:
Date: 16 October 2010, 16:05:43 + 0100
From: Maria <marieta@mail.com>
To: Juan <juanitu@mail.com>

Juan,

I can't get over it.

It's stronger than I am.

I think about the scene at the jewelry store...

When the salesgirl said Ramon "was a good customer"

And I don't have anything from that jewelry store

Bastard.

Subject: Turning the page
Date: 20 October 2010, 16:05:43 + 0100
From: Maria <marieta@mail.com>
To: Juan <juanitu@mail.com>

I talked with my friend from work. The one who wasn't able to go to Rome.

We got together after leaving work and spent hours talking.

Talking to her helped me a lot. A lot.

The truth is that I've never wanted to make friends at work, and in the end, apart from you, it's the only place I'll be able to find a shoulder to lean on.

We made plans to do something this weekend. She told me that I have to start to turn the page.

So many people have said that to me... But when she told me, I saw that it's what I have to do.

She is also lonely. And hurt.

She told me that she doesn't know what hurts more, the betrayal or the loneliness.

I understand so well...

I don't feel like writing.

I'm tired...

M.

Subject: After a storm…
Date: 24 October 2010, 16:05:43 + 0100
From: Maria <marieta@mail.com>
To: Juan <juanitu@mail.com>

… there is always calm.

This weekend did me a lot of good.

I was with my coworker Elena (it's funny—I'd never told you her name, and I've been talking to you about her for a while…). Well, I was with Elena and we did emotional "laundry."

Elena does Tai Chi and she took me to the beach first thing in the morning and we saluted the sun. The fresh air of the sea left our faces cold and salty, but I found it very pleasant.

I have to forgive Ramon. I need to keep the good memories, everything he did with and for me when we were together. What is done is done. And no one can change it.

Elena said that Rose, in the end, is practically also Ramon's widow. When I heard her say that, all of my inner calm vanished and I gave a start that didn't get past her. But she motioned to me… "Calm down, Maria, calm down…"

And when she said it again, I thought to myself that she was right. I should talk to this woman now that I've calmed down some…

You should try this Tai Chi stuff…

M.

Subject: Resuming my life…
Date: 26 October 2010, 17:15:40 + 0100
From: Maria <marieta@mail.com>
To: Juan <juanitu@mail.com>

Juan,

Today at work they started talking about going somewhere for the Immaculate Conception holiday.

And I said to count me in before asking where they were going.

I couldn't bear to spend all those days at home alone.

They said they're going to Majorca and I think that sounds fantastic.

I went a while back with Ramon, and it will be the first time I travel without him.

Without him with me, I mean.

Well, you know what I mean.

These folks from work are very friendly.

And life goes on.

M.

Subject: Resuming my life (2)
Date: 26 October 2010, 17:20:33 + 0100
From: Maria <marieta@mail.com>
To: Juan <juanitu@mail.com>

Juan!

I didn't get back to you!

I did listen to your message. And yes, yes, I'd love to go to the movies on Friday.

Well, it won't be the first time you and I go alone, will it?

Nor will it be the last.

But it will be the first time I go to the movies since...

I don't want to get sad. I've cried enough.

Let me know what time you want to meet.

And I trust you'll bring me back home...

Maria

Subject: See you tomorrow!
Date: 28 October 2010, 17:20:33 + 0100
From: Maria <marieta@mail.com>
To: Juan <juanitu@mail.com>

I got your text message.

It sounds good to me.

At the door to the theater at 7:30 p.m.

And you'll get the tickets.

Let me know what I owe you.

And don't tell me what we're going to see. Surprise me!

See you tomorrow!

M.

Subject:
Date: 30 October 2010, 10:10:45 + 0100
From: Maria <marieta@mail.com>
To: Juan <juanitu@mail.com>

Juan,

I'm embarrassed.

I'm really sorry about the number I pulled yesterday evening.

I wanted to go to the movies—I was really excited—but I guess my nerves betrayed me.

It was the first time I've gone out with you since Ramon died and I guess all of my emotions flooded me at once.

I got really nervous. Nothing like that has ever come over me before.

I thought I was suffocating and going to die.

And I don't want to die.

Forgive me, please.

Do you want to give it another go next week?

Let me know.

And thanks for everything.

Maria

Subject: Stuff...
Date: 2 November 2010, 18:20:15 + 0200
From: Maria <marieta@mail.com>
To: Juan <juanitu@mail.com>

Juan,

Yesterday was All Saints' Day. I watched as people went to the cemetery to bring flowers to their loved ones.

I have never taken flowers to either my Mom or my sister. And I have Ramon here at home.

Maybe I should take Ramon to the cemetery. So he can rest. And I would also rest since I haven't needed to touch the urn to fall asleep for days...

And I'm afraid I'll break it.

Do you think it's bad for me to think that?

M.

Subject: Tomorrow…
Date: 4 November 2010, 19:13:05 + 0200
From: Maria <marieta@mail.com>
To: Juan <juanitu@mail.com>

Juan,

Do you want to try the movies again tomorrow?

It would make me very happy.

Tell me something, please.

M.

Subject: Much better
Date: 7 November 2010, 19:55:35 + 0200
From: Maria <marieta@mail.com>
To: Juan <juanitu@mail.com>

Juan,

Thanks for giving me a chance.

I had a great time at the movies.

And I enjoyed you coming to dinner with me.

Thanks

Maria

Subject: I've decided
Date: 8 November 2010, 19:35:12 + 0200
From: Maria <marieta@mail.com>
To: Juan <juanitu@mail.com>

Juan,

I've started to see the light.

I have to call "R." I have to speak with Rose.

I have to do it.

I have to do a lot of things.

Maria

Subject: I don't know what to do...
Date: 9 November 2010, 20:33:12 + 0200
From: Maria <marieta@mail.com>
To: Juan <juanitu@mail.com>

Juan,

I'm riddled with doubts.

And I'm afraid.

What if I find I like this woman more than myself?

What do I do?

Maria

Subject: The first parcels...
Date: 11 November 2010, 19:25:31 + 0200
From: Maria <marieta@mail.com>
To: Juan <juanitu@mail.com>

Juan,

I called "R" two days ago. Rose.

It feels strange to type her name, and it hurts, but I have to do it...

I made plans with her and we met today.

It wasn't a friendly encounter because that makes no sense. There is no kind of friendship, nor will there ever be, but I had to do it.

I gave her the package from the jewelry store. After all, he bought it for her.

And really, she was also betrayed because he had her believing he was much freer than he was.

We have that in common.

We met on a park bench and you could see the car park where Ramon used to leave the car from there.

When we said goodbye (and I don't reckon we'll ever see each other again), she opened her bag to put away the little box I'd given her. And then I saw it.

The floral foulard, the one I'd misplaced and had you rummaging around in your car after. I thought I'd lost it at home or left it in your car. And suddenly the image came to me... I left it in Ramon's car.

I don't know how "R" came to have it, and I didn't ask. But it felt like an unresolved issue had been closed. I've found the foulard.

When I got home I called Ramon's brother and told him to take the car whenever they want since I won't be doing anything with it.

He got very friendly, offering to help me and all. I hung up.

I wasn't in the mood for so many excuses.

He called back and I said that that the call must have dropped. He said goodbye without any rigamarole and we both hung up.

I got rid of two parcels today.

There are still a lot left at home...

I have work to do; I still have a lot of work to do.

Speak to you soon.

Maria

Subject: End of trip
Date: 14 November 2010, 19:25:31 + 0200
From: Maria <marieta@mail.com>
To: Juan <juanitu@mail.com>

Juan,

I brought everything I'd packed up down from the attic. And I packed up more stuff from the closets.

Now there's the box from work left in the attic, R.M.P., and the gym bag.

And my closets are empty.

Like my soul.

I don't know what I'll fill them with, but I have time, lots of time, to think about it.

I called a taxi and took all the packages down.

When we went into the nursing home, the attendant let the manager know. They saw how resolute I was and what a serious look I had on my face—if they had planned a little speech of thanks not a word escaped their lips.

I left everything and have not even looked back.

Part of my life stays there. And I'm turning the page.

Afterwards I went to the cemetery in the same taxi. I rented a columbarium and I will take Ramon's ashes there. They asked me if I wanted to put an inscription and I told them just his initials: R.M.P.

Nothing else.

When I left the cemetery, I asked the taxi driver to leave me alone inside for a few minutes. I wanted to cry and I wanted to do it alone.

Poor man, he was very kind; he gave me a pack of tissues.

When I'd had enough I asked him to take me home but I stopped at the hair salon.

I asked the stylist to cut my hair, and it felt like everything went deathly silent...

I'm sure it was only me who had that feeling.

She asked me how I wanted it and I said, "short, very short"

She didn't say anything and started to cut it.

Locks of hair and tears were falling at the same time, but I had to do it.

With that I've cried all I need to cry.

Now I just have to learn how to laugh. And I guess it won't be easy.

I don't know. All of this is new, all of it...

My neck will feel cold this winter, but it will be anew feeling. And I need new things.

When I left the salon I felt a breath of fresh air on my face and noticed my neck was cold.

It's funny...

I could no longer remember the last time I'd done anything as "wild" as getting my hair cut today.

And it was good for me.

Fresh air. It's what I need.

A few days ago I told you I didn't know what I had left, that I didn't have anything left.

And I was wrong.

I have myself. And that should be enough.

I have a lot of plans for the future, Juan.

I want to tell you about them. When we see each other...

I have lived very good years. Now I want to live my remaining life well.

As one should.

Tomorrow I'm going out with people from work.

They invited me to a musical and I said yes.

But you and I will keep meeting on Fridays to go to the movies, right?

See you soon.

Maria

About the Author:

Núria Salán Ballesteros was born in Barcelona in the spring of 1963 and a few days later was brought to live in Sant Boi de Llobregat, where she has lived her whole life. Until a few years ago she lived in the Muntanyeta neighborhood, where she attended primary school and high school (Institut Joaquim Rubió i Ors) there. At 18 she began her university studies in Chemistry.

After completing her undergraduate degree with a specialization in Metallurgy, she began her career as a researcher and professor at the Polytechnic University of Catalonia (UPC) in the Department of Materials Science and Metallurgical Engineering.

Throughout her professional life she has collaborated with different teams of professors that have awarded her accolades and distinctions: the Award for Teaching Quality from the Social Council of the UPC in 2002, 2003, 2009 and 2010, the Vicens Vives distinction from the Generalitat de Catalunya in 2009 and 2010, and the honorable mention from *Ciencia en Acción* (Science in Action) in 2010.

In 2000 she was the Secretary of the First National Congress of Women and Engineering in Terrassa. She has been a collaborator in all editions of the *Programa Dona* (Women's Program) held by the UPC and in activities for promoting and introducing technological studies to high school students. Since June 2011 she has been the coordinator of UPC's Gender Program, which energizes implementation of UPC's II Equal Opportunities Plan.

Regarding her involvement in social and community affairs, she was a founding member of two associations: EQUILIBRI, the Association of Relatives and Friends of the Mentally Ill of Sant Boi and ASAMMET, the Association of Friends of Metallurgy, where she runs the secretary's office.

She is currently the secretary of the Shotokan Karate Association of Sant Boi and the Board of the Catalan Society of Technology and the treasurer of the Board of *Ciencia en Acción*. She also belongs to the Sant Boi Municipal Women's Council and participates actively in the working committees of the Baix Llobregat Women's Council.

Sant Boi writer Amadeu Alemany has captured the essence of Núria Salán in his book of interviews *Gegants (amb denominació d'origen santboiana)* where she is featured alongside Marc Gasol, Juan Carlos Pérez Rojo, Manel Esteller, Dolo Beltran and Albert Malo, among others.

Her literary interest was sparked several years ago, first bearing fruit in 2011 when she won the first prize in the Sant Joan Despí Short Story Contest with her short story *El Curs de Gestió de l'Estrès*. She translated *Des de la meva realitat*, a novel by Sant Boi writer Joan Massip, and collaborated in editing and revising the text of Sant Boi journalist Guillem Gómez Marco's book *Francesc Calvet, el pagès que va triomfar al Barça*.

With the novel *Are You Busy Friday?* She has entered a new writing stage beyond the scientific and technological sphere.